W0038064

THE CONFESSION

Sandeep has just completed his graduation in B.E. (Chemical engineering) and has been selected in a MNC for a job through campus interview.

His family consisted of his parents and he was their only son.

He was pampered by his family from his early childhood and he was good at whatever he did; be it academics, sports or co curricular activities.

His family was simple in nature and they never got involved in any duels with their neighbourhood. They had their own respect in the society and the neighbours loved them too.

Sandeep's father worked as a clerk in a government office and was about to retire in the coming four months time. He was not worried all about it as he knew that he can depend on his son for his future and his son would take care of him.

Sandeep was excited that day as it was going to be his first day in his first job of his life. He has always dreamt of giving his family the comforts, pleasures and changing the status of his family.

He woke up early that day and got dressed up after having his bath; took the blessings of his parents and had his breakfast.

He wore a light pink shirt and dark brown trousers and saw himself in the mirror. Not bad he thought to himself.

After having the breakfast he went to the bus stop where his company bus would be coming to receive him.

He stood there for half an hour when the bus arrived at the bus stop. He climbed in and saw the other staffs of the company already seated. He found a place in the last row of the bus and sat in the corner seat near the window.

The bus arrived in the company after a one hour ride from his place.

He got down and saw the campus of the company. The campus was huge enough to accommodate nearly 750 employees in a single shift.

He enquired where he should report and to whom he should report and he was shown the way to the administrative office. He went inside the office and introduced him at the reception.

The receptionist led him to another room where other students were sitting who were also excited as much as Sandeep.

He sat in the second row and gave a glimpse at the room where he was sitting.

The room was brightly lit with the walls painted in yellow color. There were two windows in the room located opposite to each other from where one could get the view of the company's campus. He was feeling the coldness as the air conditioner was on.

The room was filled with eight students who were totally freshers for the job and he could see some were known to each other and some were not. Some were talking to each other while some were sitting silently.

After some time, one employee of the company entered the room and introduced herself as Ms. Shayali who works as the HR in this company and introduced herself in brief.

She then asked for the introduction of other students.

"Good morning ma'm, I am Aarohi Saxena. I have completed my graduation in B.E. (Chemical engineering) from I.I.T. (Kanpur)".

"Good morning ma'm, I am Manoj Chauhan. I have completed my graduation in B.E. (Chemical engineering) from Vidhyabhuvan University."

"Good morning ma'm, I am Sandeep Mishra. I have completed my graduation in B.E. (Chemical engineering) from G. H. Patel College of Engineering & Technology".

One by one all the students gave their introduction. They were served with tea in the room and were told that they will be later taken to their respective desks and will be explained about their job profiles.

Sandeep was shown his desk by the HR. On his desk were placed a computer, a landline phone and some files in the corner of the cubicle.

He took his seat and he felt some energetic motivation from inside which he could not express to anyone. He was too much excited that he could not hold it any longer.

All the students were assigned their respective seats and they were given a reference book which contained details of their job profile as well as some training materials that they need to study to excel in their job.

Sandeep took the reference book in his hand and opened it.

SANDEEP MISHRA – EXECUTIVE PROJECT ENGINEER

He could not believe it. He turned the page to see the job profile. It mentioned:

1. Need to understand the basics of the project.
2. Evaluate the cost required to implement it.
3. Technically support the customer in implementing the project.
4. Need to travel to the customer's place if required for long periods of time.

There were also mentioned other details about the benefits he will receive, compensations, bonus, etc.

As it was his first day, there was no work load and the students were told to go to the canteen to have their lunch in the afternoon.

Sandeep too went with them and stood in a line for receiving the lunch. They were handed a coupon booklet from which a coupon is to be given in the canteen daily on the basis of which the lunch or tea will be served.

He handed the coupon and took his plate of lunch and sat on the table. Another person who also had joined the same day came and sat opposite to him.

"Hi, I am Aakash" he introduced himself.

"Oh, Hi, I am Sandeep." Sandeep said with a smile.

"I am from Maharashtra." Aakash continued.

"I am a Gujarati though my forefathers are from Uttar Pradesh", Sandeep replied.

Both gave the details of their family background and soon became friends in the first lunch itself.

After the lunch, all the students went back to their respective desks and began reading the reference books given related to their training.

The first day came to an end and Sandeep was too happy that his joy knew no bounds.

He could not wait to tell his parents about his new friend, about his job profile, and about his first day's experience.

He came home at 8 pm in the evening and narrated the whole day's experience to his parents who were also happy on hearing the details.

The next day Sandeep came to the office and sat in his desk and switched on the computer. He was supposed to prepare a report on what he has understood about his job profile and if he had any doubts he can ask for clarification.

He began preparing the report about his job profile in detail and mailed it to the HR.

He had understood the profile completely and did not have any doubt about it. He again began reading his reference book to understand what the contents were and how it could help him in his job. He began reading through the book and got totally engrossed in it.

At the company gate, a car arrived and the watchman opened the gates and saluted the girl sitting inside the car.

The car went inside the campus and stopped at the main entrance.

A girl in her early twenties got down and went into the office. Peons started saluting her and without giving any response, she went into her cabin.

Kritika, the daughter of the president of the company was very beautiful and whoever met her for the first time would lose his consciousness in her beauty.

On her table was a file containing the list of employees who have joined the previous day in the company.

She opened the file and began going through the names one by one.

The file also contained the details of the qualification, address, contact number and other required details and most importantly it had the photograph of the specific person.

She just wanted to see what the young guys in the company looked like and what talent they had that they were selected for the job.

She found the list boring until she came across the details of Sandeep Mishra.

She saw the photo and read the name slowly "Sandeep Mishra".

She began to like the person just by looking at the photograph but still she wanted to see how he looked like in real and what kind of person he was.

She opened the curtains of her window and saw staffs working on their own desk. She began searching for Sandeep.

She saw him in one of the desks totally absorbed in his study concentrating without talking to someone or looking somewhere else.

I need to know more about she thought but decided to proceed slowly.

It was lunch time and as usual Sandeep along with Aakash went to the canteen to have his lunch. They both decided to sit on the same table where they had their lunch yesterday.

The peon brought Kritika's lunch and was about to serve when she ordered him to take the lunch to the canteen and she would be having her lunch there. The peon too was surprised to hear this because he knew that she never had her lunch in the canteen as she hated the crowd present in the canteen.

As ordered, the peon took her lunch to the canteen and she followed him to the canteen.

She sat beside the table where Sandeep and Aakash were sitting and gossiping while having their lunch.

She decided to listen to their talk and ate her lunch silently.

"Hey, look at the menu. The food is delicious today too." said Aakash.

"Of course, even yesterday the lunch was good and it tastes good today also." replied Sandeep.

Just when they were having their lunch, Aakash saw a beautiful girl sitting on the table next to them.

"Sandeep, do you see a beautiful girl sitting beside us? What do you think of her?" asked Aakash.

Sandeep was surprised for a moment as he could not understand what Aakash wanted to say to him.

"See, I am not here to date girls and admire their beauty. I am here to work. That's it." saying this he left his table after completing his lunch.

He went back to his table and resumed his work again.

Kritika was little disappointed as Sandeep did not speak a single word about her. This was the first time ever when a boy has ignored her. She had already received many proposals earlier; either she would ignore it or reject it without any second thought.

She came back to her cabin and opened the curtain again and saw Sandeep concentrating too much than required on the work. She could not understand why he did so like that.

On that day, a party was arranged by the company for the new comers and all the staffs were also invited.

Sandeep called Aakash and asked if he was to go the party and if he goes then to pick him up from his home.

Aakash told Sandeep to be ready by 7:30 pm.

Sandeep got ready and wore a red shirt and a black trousers and a golden wrist watch.

He was looking more handsome than what he used to look in his official formal clothes. He came downstairs and called Aakash to enquire where he was and he got reply that Aakash would arrive in just five minutes time and was told to come near the gate.

But before Sandeep reached the gate, Aakash already reached there on his bike.

Sandeep sat at the pillion and they both left for the party.

The party plot was in the company campus itself and was a little bigger such that it could accommodate all the staffs.

Sandeep and Aakash entered the party venue and went inside the hall where the party was arranged.

They were welcomed by their seniors and when they entered the room, a fragrance of sweet smelling roses filled in the air welcomed them.

The room was lit dimly with yellow lights on the ceiling. The room was cool as the air conditioner was running at 22^0C. There were tables arranged in a systematic manner with white clothes covered on the chairs.

There were food items arranged, with music going on and also wines were provided to the staffs.

Sandeep had never been to this kind of party before.

Sandeep and Aakash came together and sat on one of the table and were looking around seeing what others were doing.

Kritika came and started searching for Sandeep. She soon spotted him with Aakash and decided not to go to Sandeep in the presence of Aakash.

The party began at around 8 pm in the evening.

On one side DJ was going on and the youngsters were enjoying it like anything. On the other side the dinner was served.

Kritika was wearing red miniskirt and was looking totally different on that day.

Aakash saw Kritika from distance and told to Sandeep, "See, the same girl who sat beside our table today during the lunch. She looks really beautiful."
Sandeep ignored his saying and was looking elsewhere.

Aakash saw that Kritika was staring at Sandeep from distance.

"I tell you that the girl to whom I am referring is staring at you now." told Aakash.

"Can't you keep quiet for a moment?" saying this Sandeep turned his face towards the direction where Aakash was looking.

Yes, Kritika was looking at Sandeep.

She started walking towards Sandeep and came to the place where Sandeep and Aakash were sitting together.

"Hi, I am Kritika Sharma. I am too working in the same office where you two are working. I am working here as Personal secretary to the president of the company." she said forwarding her hand for a handshake.

Sandeep too shook his hands and with a smile introduced himself.

Aakash too was waiting to see her next move but she left the place without saying a word to Aakash.

The youngsters were dancing to the songs and the hall will filled with total happiness and enjoyment as the new comers were shouting and dancing along with their friends.

Aakash too wanted to dance but not alone. He wanted someone to accompany him.

He asked Sandeep if he could come with him but Sandeep refused saying that he is not good at dancing.

Aakash was disappointed a little but said nothing and went to the bar to have some drinks.

Sandeep too sat beside him but he did not have a drink too as he was not used to it.

Kritika after sometime again came to Sandeep.

"Hey, wanna dance?" she asked.

"No, I am not good at dancing." replied Sandeep immediately.

Kritika still insisted him to dance but he kept on refusing. Aakash wanted to join Kritika but he did not dare to ask her as he felt if he asked her directly then she may reject him.

Kritika kept her hands on Sandeep's palm. He looked at her and moved his hands away.

"See, there is nothing in it. You can dance with me. We are friends. Are we not?" asked Kritika.

Sandeep smiled and replied, "See, I told you I am not good at it. To be more frank, I am not used to this kind of parties. I have just come here as an employee's participation and nothing else. Please leave me alone."

Kritika left the place without saying a word as she had not expected this from him. The disappointment could be seen in her face.

"Why did you refuse her? After all she just asked you to dance with her." asked Aakash.

"Is it? If you want to dance with her, you are free to go. I did not stop you from going with her. I just told that I am not used to these kinds of parties so I don't want to dance. That's it. And I don't think it is mandatory to dance in these parties." replied Sandeep.

Aakash made a face towards Sandeep which he ignored.

"Have you finished your drinks? If yes, then we can leave." Sandeep said.

Kritika again came this time but not to meet Sandeep. Instead she ordered some drinks for her and started drinking.

Sandeep saw all this and was surprised. He could not believe that the girl who introduced herself to him drinks.

He pointed this to Aakash but Aakash did not show any interest this time.

"So what is new in this if she is drinking? Even women drink nowadays. I don't think there is nothing wrong in it." he replied.

"But still I don't think it is correct according to Indian culture." Sandeep spoke again. Aakash did not reply this time and asked Sandeep if he wanted to go home or have some more time at the party.

Sandeep wished to go home and both of them left the place.

"You are drunk. You should not drive." said Sandeep.

"SShhh, keep quiet. I know what to do and what not to do. You just sit in the pillion silently. I will drop you at your home." replied Aakash.

Without saying anything Sandeep sat beside and Aakash drove off.

The cold wind was blowing towards them and it was darker with no lights on the street.

Aakash drove at a speed of 80 km/hr and that too in a drunken state. Sandeep asked him to slow down his speed but to no avail.

The speed became uncontrollable and his bike hit a large boulder on the side of the road and both of them were thrown away in the air and they landed in different directions.

Both of them shouted for help but the road was totally empty with no pedestrians nearby.

After nearly an hour, a car approached on that way and the driver in the car spotted them and came to their rescue.

Aakash was bleeding from his neck as an iron rod has pierced through his neck while Sandeep was hit on the head by the rocks lying around. He was bleeding on his head as well as on his hands.

An ambulance was called and both of them were hospitalized and their parents were informed.

Sandeep's parents came to the hospital and saw their son admitted in the I.C.U and he was still unconscious. They were informed that he had been hit on the head and needs a surgery immediately.

They signed the documents and Sandeep was immediately shifted to the operation theatre.

Aakash had got his hand fractured and too was taken for the surgery.

Parents of both Sandeep and Aakash were waiting outside the operation theatre anxiously for the surgery to end.

The doctor who operated Aakash came out of operation first.

"Is my son ok?" asked Aakash's mother to the doctor.

"Yes, nothing critical. He will be fine in next two days." replied the doctor.

After nearly two hours, the doctor who operated Sandeep came out and he too was bombarded with the same questions by Sandeep's parents.

"Nothing can be said at present. We can only say about his condition after 24 hours." replied the doctor and went away.

Sandeep's mother started crying and his father consoled her and told to her to have trust in God.

Sandeep was again shifted to I.C.U. after the surgery and his parents were not allowed to sit beside him. They sat the whole night on the lobby outside the I.C.U. with his mother still crying looking through the glass door expecting her son to regain consciousness.

The next morning, Sandeep's and Aakash's issue reached their company.

Kritika came to office as usual and saw through the window that Sandeep has not come to office that day.

Her phone rang at the same time. She picked up the phone and answered the call. It was her dad.

"Hello dad", she said

"Hello, my dear", replied her father and continued, "I called you to inform that two of our employees; Sandeep and Aakash have met with an accident after they left the party and have been hospitalized. Both of them have undergone surgery now."

"What? Are you sure?" asked Kritika who was in a shock by now.

"Yes, it is a confirmed information." replied her father.

"Tell me the name of hospital and I will visit them." told Kritika.

"They have been admitted at Bombay Hospital." replied her father.

Kritika immediately kept the phone down, took her bag and locked her cabin and called the driver to get the car ready.

The car came and she drove off to Bombay Hospital.

She reached the hospital in half an hour and soon was at the reception of the hospital.

"Excuse me, may I know what the room number is where Sandeep and Aakash are admitted?" she asked the receptionist.

"Yes madam. Sandeep is admitted in I.C.U while Aakash is admitted in room number 402." replied the receptionist.

Kritika hurriedly went to the I.C.U. first and saw Sandeep's parents sitting out at a desk in the lobby.

She went nearby and stood nearby Sandeep's mother.

"Aunty, I am Kritika and I am working with Sandeep." she introduced herself.

"I would like to meet Sandeep." she continued.

"He is still unconscious and is not responding at all." replied his mother and showed her the way to I.C.U.

Kritika went to the doors of I.C.U. and peeped in through a mini glass that gave view of patient from outside.

Sandeep was fully bandaged on his head and his hand was also fully bandaged. Tubes were connected to his nose and also oxygen was supplied to him through oxygen cylinders.

He did not move even an inch and lay on the bed still as if he is dead.

Tears began to flow through Kritika's eyes. This was not the condition she wished to see Sandeep.

She entered the I.C.U. and went near the bed. She could feel the pain Sandeep was going through but the difference was she could speak it out at the moment while Sandeep could not.

She bent forward and held his hand on hers.

"Sandeep, I want you back the way you were. Please wake up soon. I don't want to see you like this anymore." she said when drops of her tears fell on Sandeep's palms but he still did not respond and lay motionless.

Unable to see him anymore, she left the I.C.U. ward and went to see Aakash in the upper floor; room number 402.

She knocked the door and opened it a little.

She saw Aakash sitting on the bed with no one nearby and was bandaged around his neck.

She entered in and Aakash could not believe his eyes.

"Welcome Ms??" said Aakash doubtedly.

"Ms. Kritika." replied Kritika.

"Are you not the same girl who were sitting beside our table during the lunch break in the canteen as well as who met us during the party?" asked Aakash.

"Yes, I am the same girl." said Kritika.

"How do you feel now?" enquired Kritika.

"Better than before but still it pains in the neck." replied Aakash.

"How did you met with the accident?" Kritika asked again to know exactly what happened on that night.

Aakash narrated the whole incident from Sandeep declining to allow him to drive; to meeting with the accident and later getting admitted to the hospital.

"When you were drunk, then why did you drive?" asked Kritika angrily.

"Who knew that we were destined to meet with this fate?" said Aakash smiling.

"Don't smile. I am serious. Have you seen the condition Sandeep is? He has still not regained consciousness." shouted Kritika.

"I too feel sorry about it. I feel guilt too. I have offered to help his parents but they refused stating that I am not at fault." replied Aakash.

Kritika made up her mind and decided to fund Sandeep's hospital expenses without his or his parent's knowledge.

She met the doctor who was attending Sandeep and told him about her idea to pay Sandeep's expenses and send the bill directly to the company instead of asking for payment from his parents.

Kritika then left back to office but on that day she could not concentrate on her work as the condition of Sandeep was bothering her.

Whenever she thought of Sandeep, tears would flow down her eyes without her knowledge.

Two days later, Sandeep regained his consciousness.

When he opened his eyes, he saw his parents standing beside him and his mother was still crying with happiness. Also Aakash was discharged by this time and he had come from his home to meet him.

Sandeep tried to sit but was asked not to do so by the doctor as he still needed some bed rest.

Kritika too came to know of the news and she made her second visit to the hospital.

By this time, Sandeep was shifted to the special ward from the I.C.U.

Sandeep felt as if he is seeing the world after a long period of time and has taken a rebirth. He felt everything new, the taste of food that his mother had cooked for him, the people around him, the sounds his ears heard and many more.

Kritika came to his room and knocked the door.

"May I come in?" she asked.

"Oh yes, come in." replied Sandeep's mother welcoming her in

She came inside and saw Sandeep lay on the bed but still awake.

"How do you feel now?" she asked.

Sandeep saw her as if he is seeing her for the first time and did not respond for a second. He soon recognized her.

"Yes, I am fine now." he replied.

Kritika had brought some eatables and fruits for him and handed it to his mother.

She sat beside Sandeep telling him about the happenings in the office and how the others felt his absence.

"I will resume soon once I am discharged from the hospital." told Sandeep.

"Not so early. You can take your own time. Don't be in a hurry to resume your job." said Kritika and got ready to leave.

"She is really a sweet girl and also kind hearted." said Sandeep's mother to him.

Sandeep did not say anything and was silent.

Kritika went to the doctor again and asked him about Sandeep discharge and was told that he would be discharged within next week once all the results of the tests to be conducted would come out as positive.

Kritika also enquired about the bill details and reminded the doctor to send the bill to the company rather than giving it to Sandeep's parents.

Days passed and Sandeep was much better by now and the result of the tests conducted on him showed positive results which meant he had progressed a lot.

"Tomorrow morning you will be discharged." said the doctor during one of the regular visits to Sandeep.

"At least now I can see the open world doctor." said Sandeep jokingly.

Sandeep was eager to get discharged from the hospital so that he could resume back to his job.

The next morning the doctor arrived on his regular rounds and told Sandeep to get ready for discharge.

Kritika was waiting at the reception to receive the bill and told the receptionist to handover the bill to her instead of Sandeep's parents.

After some time the bill was handed to Kritika. The total amount to be paid was Rs. 1,25,000/- which included the cost of surgery, tests and other things.

She paid the bill in cheque and left the hospital in a hurry.

Sandeep's parents came to collect the bill from the reception and they were told that the bill has already been paid.

They enquired about whom had paid but was told that the person had requested the hospital not to reveal the name.

Sandeep came home and sat on the couch to watch television. He switched on the TV and was watching news when his mobile phone rang.

"Hello, Sandeep here." he responded.

"Hello, Kritika here." came the reply.

"Hi, I may come to the office by day after tomorrow." told Sandeep.

"Not so early. You can take your own time as I said before." replied Kritika.

"But my mind ponders over the office rather than at home. I can't wait more than this." Sandeep insisted.

"OK. It's up to you. You may come." told Kritika.

On the appointed day, Sandeep went to his office. He felt as if he was in a new atmosphere, in a new place and among new people.

All the staffs gathered around Sandeep to ask him about his health.

After informing them, Sandeep sat on his table. The phone on his table rang.

"Hello, Sandeep here." he said receiving the call.

"Hello, Mr. Sharma here." said the voice on the other side and asked him to meet him in his cabin.

He went to Mr. Sharma's room.

Mr. Sharma enquired about his health and told him that he has got something important to share with him.

Sandeep could not make out what it was and was eager to know why he was called for.

Mr. Sharma began.

"Our company has got a project installation order in USA and our company has decided to send you to USA along with another colleague."

Sandeep was happy on hearing this and his joy knew bounds. He didn't know what to say. He just said thank you his boss and went back to his table smiling and dreaming of being in a new city soon.

He called his home and told his mother about this issue.

On the other hand, Kritika felt sad as she could not think of working in office without looking at Sandeep.

She asked her father to send her too even though there were no reason for it. Her father could not understand why she asked for it but assured her if required she would be sent too.

On knowing about his trip, Sandeep's colleagues congratulated him as they knew it was a rare opportunity and that too for a new colleague.

Sandeep soon updated his status on facebook and soon there were many 'likes' and 'comments' congratulating him.

Sandeep began searching for homes through online portal to reside in USA. He wanted a one room BHK home and that too cheaper ones. He posted an ad as per his requirement and waited to get response.

His preparation to go to USA was in full swing. On one side he was busy with his office work and on other side he made plans of his life in USA.

Kritika saw him too much excited one day and asked him why he was so much excited.

"Being born in a middle class family, the opportunity that I have got now is rare. In fact, I call it a golden opportunity as it knocks the door once in a lifetime. Who knows what God has got in store for me ahead?" said Sandeep.

He was posted at Illinois, California for a period of two years. He was supposed to support the customer in technical issues.

Only two days were left for him to depart to USA. At his home, relatives from faraway visited him. He sometimes doubted if they came to his home just to see him off or was it really they wanted to meet him for something else.

Aakash always nowadays spent time with Sandeep as he knew they will now meet only after two years. Sandeep and Aakash always went together wherever they went either be it shopping or having lunch or dinner.

The day finally arrived.

Sandeep was fully excited as he was going to have his maiden trip to a foreign land.

His family came with him to send him off at the airport. Aakash too was with him to see him off.

Kritika called Sandeep to wish him a happy journey. It was after all she who pressurized her father to send him to USA as she had her own plans for him.

Sandeep landed at the California airport after a twenty two hour journey. The cool breeze of the country welcomed him as he came out of the airport.

Michael, one of his colleagues in USA was waiting for him at the airport to receive him.

Both of them travelled in a taxi to his home which was allotted to him by the company.

Sandeep was astonished by the tall buildings all through the way. The displays of hoardings on the roadside amazed him.

"You look so excited." told Michael.

"Yes, this is my first visit outside India." replied Sandeep.

After an hour journey, Sandeep came to his home and keeping his baggage down he gave a look around.

A painting was hung on the wall which displayed a girl collecting flowers from the forest at the time of evening.

The girl was dressed in a white top and a red frock with a scarf on her and a basket in her hand.

"I love it." he said looking at a painting displayed on the wall.

"What you love? The painting or the girl in the painting" asked Michael.

Sandeep looked at him not knowing why he asked it.

"I love the painting; not the girl and I mean it." he replied changing his tone.

"OK OK. Cool. I was just kidding." replied Michael.

"By the way, I am coming to office tomorrow." continued Sandeep changing the topic of discussion.

"Oh sure, I will come and pick you up at 9 Am." said Michael getting ready to leave Sandeep's place.

After Michael left, Sandeep sat on the couch for a moment. He felt homesick now. He called back his home and informed his parents about his journey.

They were happy to hear that he has reached USA safely.

Sandeep did not go outside for dinner that evening but instead just had biscuits which he had brought from India and felt asleep.

Early morning he woke up when the alarm rang at 5:30 am.

At first he could not recognize where he was and kept looking on the ceiling lying on the bed.

He got up from his bed and sat on the bed for two minutes and went to get ready to his office.

He got ready by 8 am and went to the balcony.

His home was on the 8th floor. He saw cars moving around down the street. People were busy down the lane. Some were going to office, while some were bidding good bye to their children.

After some time his phone rang. It was Michael.

"Hello, Michael here. Are you ready?" he asked.

"Yes, I am. You may come now." replied Sandeep.

It was not ten minutes before Michael came and rang his door bell. Sandeep welcomed him.

"Enjoyed yesterday night's sleep?" asked Michael.

"Yes, I did." replied Sandeep asking Michael to sit down on the couch.

"Come on. Let's go to the hotel first, have some breakfast and then we will go to office." told Michael.

Both Sandeep and Michael left in Michael's car.

They reached a hotel at the outskirts of the city. "HOTEL MILLIONS" the board read.

"Hotel Millions. Is it only for millionaires?" asked Sandeep jokingly.

"Nice question. Even I need to ask them for explanation." replied Michael smiling.

Both entered the hotel.

The hotel was dark inside with tables arranged in a nice manner. Sandeep's eyes began looking through the hotel making a guess about what he was going to have for breakfast.

On the right was a bar inside a hotel where drinks were available of different varieties.

"What you like to have?" asked Michael.

"Anything purely vegetarian." replied Sandeep.

"Oh my god. You a pure vegetarian?" exclaimed Michael in a surprise.

Sandeep did not understand why Michael took it by surprise and asked him what was wrong in being a pure vegetarian.

"In USA, you rarely find pure vegetarians. Even a vegetarian eats eggs here and I hope you are aware of that." continued Michael.

"They may be. But I don't." Sandeep shot back.

"You think it is wrong to be a non vegetarian?" asked Michael.

"You think it is wrong to be a vegetarian?" asked back Sandeep.

"Well, I think at least in USA you should have non vegetarian foods. You may not get better non vegetarian dishes other than here. I suggest you to at least taste some." continued Michael.

"Definitely not. I am not brought up by eating non vegetarian dishes. Even my parents don't have it. So I think even I should not." told Sandeep.

"Your parents belong to a different generation than what you are. You are in a MNC and in a modern society. At least I suggest you should eat it though your parents may or may not approve of it." said Michael.

Sandeep lost his temper trying to convince Michael. He got up from his chair and went out to the car.

"Hey wait. Listen to me. I didn't mean it by the way." Michael shouted following Sandeep and convinced him to come inside to have the breakfast.

"You will not decide what I should eat and what I should not. Understand? I know it well." said Sandeep in an angry tone.

"It's ok. You are free to do so." said Michael and called the waiter to give them the menu card.

The menu card had various dishes listed on it.

It mostly contained the non vegetarian dishes and vegetarian dishes were scarcely available.

"I prefer to only have coffee and no dishes." said Sandeep to waiter ordering for a coffee.

"Are you sure you don't want to eat anything?" asked Michael.

"I don't want to risk myself ordering any non vegetarian dish by mistake." replied Sandeep.

Michael ordered an egg sandwich for him along with a cocoa drink.

Sandeep silently drank his coffee and asked Michael to finish his breakfast earlier so that he could go to office early instead of being late on the first day itself.

Soon Michael finished his breakfast and both of them left for the office.

It was an hour journey from the hotel to office and both of them reached the office gate at 10:15 am.

Michael accompanied Sandeep inside and started introducing him to other colleagues.

"This is Starc, working here as a quality analyst", said Michael to a colleague who was taller than Sandeep.

Sandeep shook hands with him with a smile and introduced himself to him.

"This is Lisa, working here as a chemist." said Michael pointing to a girl in her blue top and black trousers.

"This is Katherine. She is in the production department." concluded Michael and said he will be introduced to many more when the time will come.

Sandeep expressed his joy to meet his new colleagues and asked about his work place. He was shown his cabin where he was about to start his work in a new place amongst new people.

Sandeep entered his cabin. On the door was a name plate mentioning his name along with his job title.

He opened the door of his cabin.

The cabin was big enough to accommodate nearly ten to twelve people. On the center of the room was a table with a computer on it and also were some files neatly arranged in a nicely manner.

Sandeep closed the door and gave a look around his cabin. On the wall he found the same painting which he saw at his home.

He thought perhaps this picture has got something to do with this company. May be at other staffs home too he could find the same painting.

He went and drew opened the curtain which hung behind his chair.

The sun rays entered the cabin brightening it more than before.

He sat on his chair. He was supposed to go for a site visit the next day for installing a process and he was well aware of it.

He called Michael to his cabin.

Michael came and sat before him.

"Well, I need the details of the site that we are visiting tomorrow for the installation of the process." he said directly coming to the matter.

"You need to talk to Katherine for that as she knows for what product the installation is to be done. I will send her in." said Michael and left the room.

Within moments, Katherine entered.

"Sir, here is the details you asked for." she said handling him a file which contained the product details and the installation required to be done on the site.

"What is the cost value of this project?" asked Sandeep.

"$ 24,00,000" came the reply from Katherine.

"Who else is going to accompany me tomorrow?" asked Sandeep.

"Michael, Me and a colleague from India will be accompanying you." Katherine said.

"A colleague from India? Who?" asked Sandeep in a surprise.

"Kritika Sharma, coming tonight." Katherine said.

"Is she coming here? She never told me about this." Sandeep said standing up from his chair.

"Yes, she is going to join you on your USA trip." said Katherine smiling.

"Ok, you may go now." Sandeep said and sat silently on his chair thinking about the reason behind Kritika's arrival.

He went through the file and studied about the installation process and what the company is expecting regarding the production quality.

He knew well how to handle this installation though he had not practically dealt with in while in India.

It was lunch break now and Sandeep came out of his cabin and looked around to see most of them leaving their seats to have lunch.

"Hey, come let's go and have ours." said Michael waving his hand in air.

Sandeep went along with Michael to the company canteen.

He had his lunch and came back to his cabin to make plans about the installation process and completed it by evening.

Later in the evening, Michael dropped him at home and asked about his dinner.

"I am planning to skip my dinner tonight." said Sandeep.

Michael left Sandeep's home.

Sandeep soon slept.

The next morning as usual Sandeep got ready and waited for Michael to come and pick him up.

Michael came as usual and picked up Sandeep and left for the office.

Sandeep entered the cabin and opened the door.

"Welcome Mr. Sandeep Mishra." said Kritika in a different welcoming tone.

She was facing the window with her back towards the door.

"When did you come?" asked Sandeep.

"Yesterday night. How's your work going on here?" enquired Kritika.

"Fine. I didn't expect you to be here." said Sandeep trying to ask the purpose of Kritika's arrival.

"Is that so? I thought you loved surprises. So I didn't inform you while you were in India." said Kritika smiling.

"It is generally the girls who love surprises not the boys. I mean especially the boys of my kind who are workaholic." said Sandeep talking straight to the point.

"Anyway now I am here. We will be handling the project together." said Kritika.

"Where do you stay?" asked Sandeep again when Kritika was about to leave his cabin.

"In the apartment next to where you live." replied Kritika and left the cabin.

Sandeep continued his work and got ready to go to the site for project.

He called Michael and Katherine and told them to be ready in ten minutes as they have to leave for the site.

Both of them got ready on the appointed time and Sandeep came downstairs. Kritika was standing near the reception.

"What are you doing here? Don't you wanna come?" asked Sandeep.

"Of course, I am coming." replied Kritika and took her handbag and came along with them.

Michael sat on the driver's seat to drive the car. Sandeep went to sit beside him when Katherine interrupted him.

"Sir, you may sit at the back along with Kritika ma'm." she said.

"Why? I prefer to sit in front." replied Sandeep trying not to lose his temper.

"Come on Sandeep, you can sit with me. Any problem?" asked Kritika.

"No, nothing." said Sandeep giving an angry look at Katherine.

While on drive, Michael turned on his musical stereo.

A song named "I Love You" started playing.

Katherine smiled lightly looking in the front mirror.

Kritika looked at Sandeep through the mirror but he was sitting as if he was not listening to the song.

"You hearing the song?" asked Kritika.

"No. I am not interested in it." replied Sandeep.

"But why? Any reason?" asked Kritika again.

"My mind is hovering around the installation and I don't feel like listening to songs at present." shot back Sandeep.

"Be cool. There is nothing wrong in listening to songs until you reach the site." said Kritika trying to arouse the interest in Sandeep.

But all the efforts failed. He sat silently showing no effect to anything.

They reached the site after two hours journey.

They reached the gate. The security guards checked them as per the protocol and let them in.

"Welcome to our company all." said the manager Mr. Peter Groggins welcoming them inside to his cabin.

"We are very much interested in installing this line. In fact the benefits the company will be getting once the process begins by this line is unimaginable." he said to them.

"Yes, sir. I understand. Actually we need to do study the site first which will give us a basic idea of the location and the other requirements if any." said Sandeep.

The peon was called by this time and he brought a cup of tea for all along with some snacks.

The snacks consisted of some pizzas and sandwiches.

Sandeep doubted it of being a non vegetarian dish and gave a doubtful look at Kritika.

She saw him and understood what he wanted to ask her and indicated that it was a non vegetarian dish.

Sandeep just drank the tea and ignored the dish. He in fact wanted to go to the site for installation instead of simply discussing the issues.

After the tea session completed, all went to the location where the line was to be installed.

"This is the place where we wish to install the line." said Peter.

"This side is facing the north." replied Sandeep looking the vastu.

"What?" asked Mr. Peter unable to understand what Sandeep meant.

"No, nothing. I was just saying. Forget it." replied Sandeep trying to change the topic.

Kritika gave an angry look at Sandeep because she understood what he meant but said nothing.

Michael and Katherine were looking at the discussion going on between Sandeep and Peter.

They were just supposed to assist Sandeep and Kritika.

Sandeep made a list of tests that was needed to be conducted before the installation of line and asked Katherine to do the tests and prepare a report on the same.

Katherine took the list from him and gave a look at it.

It contained various tests like testing of chlorides in water, all utilities available as provided in the list and others.

Katherine got into work along with Michael who helped Katherine in doing the tests.

Once the tests were completed, a report was prepared as asked and was given to Sandeep.

Sandeep went through the results and after a brief discussion with Mr. Peter; he proceeded to the installation of the line.

He wanted to install a pilot plant in the company through which the company could calculate the rate of production that could be produced on per month basis.

It took two days for Sandeep before he completed the installation of the line.

Sandeep asked Peter to allot him some employees who are going to run the line in the future. He wanted to train them perfectly.

Peter summoned two employees and introduced them to Sandeep.

Sandeep told them the purpose of installing the line and the benefits along with its working principle.

The two employees were too interested in learning the new process. All went fine for the first two weeks.

It was February and USA was busy preparing itself for Valentine's Day.

It was a much awaited day by the youngsters in the country.

Kritika too was excited to celebrate Valentine's Day and she decided to propose Sandeep on that day.

She planned a surprise for him and took help of Michael and Katherine in executing it.

The previous night before Valentine's Day, Sandeep left early to home as he had some work related to the project going on the site.

Kritika stayed back at office along with Michael and Katherine.

She told Michael and Katherine to decorate the room of Sandeep with flowers all over the cabin.

Red roses were brought and were decorated fully such that the room was filled up with the fragrance of rose.

She wrote a letter to Sandeep expressing her love to him:

Dear Sandeep,

I know you are very workaholic. But still I believe you should have time to spend life of your own.

You need to care for people around you. You may not know there are people who care about you other than your parents.

Yes, I am saying about myself. I care for you the way I care for my family.

I don't know how to tell but whenever I see you, my heart skips a beat. In fact, I like you very much that I could openly say that I love you.

I want you to be mine always. I want to spend the rest of my life with you.

With regards,

She didn't write the name as she feared he may not accept her.

The next day as usual Sandeep came and opened the door.

The moment he opened, the fragrance of roses welcomed him by entering his nose.

He doubted if he had entered the wrong room and came out to see the name plate attached on the door.

He saw his name on the door which meant he had entered the right cabin.

He went inside and closed the door and gave his cabin a look. The whole cabin was filled with roses.

He didn't know who to ask regarding who had done this. He called Michael to his cabin.

Michael came to his room and while coming he told Kritika about the call.

"Michael, I want to know who had done this." Sandeep asked with a stern voice.

"Who did what?" asked Michael as if he did not understand anything.

"These decorations is what I am talking of." said Sandeep again.

"See, today is Valentine's Day and you know it. So why does this decorations bother you?" asked Michael again.

"Valentine's Day is not what bothering me. I want to know who did this and why. I demand an answer whoever has done it." he said shouting at Michael.

Michael sat silently not knowing what to say.

"Come on, say something. Silence is not the answer I demanded." spoke Sandeep.

"Well, there is a girl in our office who loves you and wants to propose you today. She is afraid of you not accepting her. So she planned to give you a surprise in this manner." told Michael softly.

"What? A girl loves me? Don't joke." said Sandeep as he knew no one dared to talk to him in that sense.

"Of course. I am telling the truth which may seem to be a joke to you." replied Michael.

"I wish to see the girl immediately." said Sandeep.

"Are you going to accept her?" asked Michael.

Sandeep gave an anger look at him and Michael understood what he wanted to convey. So he left the room silently.

Kritika called Michael and enquired regarding what happened in Sandeep's cabin.

He told her in detail about the discussion that went on between Sandeep and him.

"I see. Let me handle this. I know he will understand and accept me." said Kritika and went to Sandeep's cabin.

Before Kritika entered his room, Sandeep read the letter and that triggered his anger more and he believed it has got no purpose for him.

She opened the door of the cabin and immediately Sandeep saw her. She could see the anger in her eyes.

"What do you want?" asked Sandeep.

"I want to talk to you for just five minutes." replied Kritika.

"Anything of importance?" again asked Sandeep.

"Yes, it is more important than anything for me." said Kritika.

"Go ahead." Sandeep said and listened to her.

Kritika began to talk.

"Why are you like this? I want to know today." she began with a question.

"What do you mean?" enquired Sandeep raising his eyebrows.

"You scolded Michael because he told you that a girl in our office loved you?" she asked.

"He told you about what we discussed here? Stupid fellow." said Sandeep angrily.

"What's wrong in it? He is our colleague after all." she said back in anger tone.

"What do you want to say? I just want to know about the girl who had written this letter me." said Sandeep giving the letter to Kritika.

"Cool Sandeep. I will tell you who has written it." said Kritika.

"You know who it is?" asked Sandeep in a surprise.

"Yes, because it is me who has written that." said Kritika.

"What? Was it you?" shouted Sandeep.

"Yes, but listen to me first. Let me speak. I want to talk to you regarding this." continued Kritika.

Sandeep said nothing.

Kritika continued.

"The matter written in the letter is cent percent true. I mean it. I want to spend my life with you. Why don't you understand me?" said Kritika in a single breath.

"Get out." is all what Sandeep could say in reply.

Kritika left the room hurriedly as tears went down through her eyes.

Her plans for the Valentine's Day were spoilt. She expected something special but unexpected things happened.

She told Katherine that she had some work and has to leave now and left the office.

"What's the matter?" asked Katherine but without replying Kritika left.

Sandeep could not concentrate in his work that day. He felt disturbed with what had occurred between Kritika and him. He never knew she had feelings for him.

After lunch Sandeep felt too much disturbed. He simply dozed off in his cabin when his phone rang.

"Hello, Sandeep here", he answered.

"Hello, Peter here." came the voice from other side of the phone.

"Yes, sir." continued Sandeep.

"Sir, actually there is some problems going on with the line. Our men could not find out the reason and solve it on their own. We want you to help us please." Peter

"Sure sir, is it OK if I come tomorrow?" asked Sandeep.

"Yes, no problem." replied Peter.

Already he was disturbed and this phone call disturbed him more.

That night Sandeep could not eat or sleep properly and he suffered from a headache.

The whole day's incidence kept on whirling in his mind again and again though Sandeep tried to forget it, he couldn't.

Next day, Sandeep got ready to go to the site and informed Michael to be ready with Katherine.

"Even we should take Kritika with us." prompted Michael.

"No need for that. Just do as I say." said Sandeep.

The three of them left to the site leaving Kritika behind at the office.

They reached the site. Sandeep got into work immediately after a brief discussion with Mr. Peter.

Sandeep began by checking the parameters of the line and found it to be correct. He asked Katherine to get the analysis done so that he could find out where the problem was.

She did the analysis and it showed good result.

Sandeep could not make out where the error was. The problem was about the pressure that got built up in the line during the ongoing of the process. He didn't know how to reduce the pressure.

"Shall we ask Kritika? Maybe she knows how to do it?" said Michael.

"No need for that. You think I can't solve this issue?" said Sandeep.

Michael said nothing.

Sandeep went to Mr. Peter.

"Sir, I need some more time as I could not understand where the problem is coming from. I am sure I will be able to solve it. All I need is time." he said.

"You may take your own time but we expect you to solve it earlier as possible as we could not wait for longer period." said Peter.

"Yes sir. I will." replied Sandeep and left the site along with Michael and Katherine.

While on the way back, Michael began the conversation.

"Sandeep, you think what you did yesterday was correct?" he began.

"What I did yesterday? What are you talking about?" asked Sandeep.

"I mean the Kritika's issue." Michael replied softly.

Sandeep gave a stern look at Michael as he did not wish to talk about this issue any more.

"I think we should have contacted Kritika for the problem we are facing at the site." Katherine interrupted.

Sandeep sat silent this time and decided not to speak anything as the conversation was getting deeper.

They reached the office by evening and most of the staffs have now left for home.

"Michael, meet me at the bar." said Sandeep.

"When?" asked Michael.

"At 8 pm." replied Sandeep and left for home.

Michael wondered why Sandeep called him to the bar as Sandeep never drank.

Both of them met at the appointed time.

"Michael, I called you here to discuss the issue we are facing at the site." began Sandeep.

"Yes, I know." said Michael.

"I don't know exactly what is causing the problem. I am not able to make out the reason to solve it." continued Sandeep.

"We can deal it. Just have patience." said Michael.

"How can we deal it? That is what I want to know." said Sandeep

Just as both of them were discussing about the problem, a voice interrupted them by saying, "Why don't you try to open the valve located below the pipeline?"

Both of them looked upwards to see who it was.

The voice was of a girl who was in her mid twenties. The important thing was she looked Indian.

Sandeep looked at her for a moment.

"You could try that. May be that will solve the problem." she said again.

Sandeep thought as why did that idea not struck him before.

"May I know your name please?" he asked.

"I am Yutika." she replied.

"Yutika..!!! Hmm. Nice name." said Sandeep.

He continued, "Were you listening to our conversation?"

"Initially I was not interested but as it included technical issues, I took interest in it and listened to the discussion going on between you and him." Yutika said pointing her fingers towards Michael.

"May I know what is your qualification and what are you doing in this bar?" enquired Sandeep.

"I have done B.S in Chemical science. I am working here as a bearer as I didn't get any job related to my field." replied Yutika.

"I see. I will try out what you have said and will let you know for sure." said Sandeep.

Next day, Sandeep again went to the site along with Michael and Katherine.

He went to the line directly and reached the pipeline sector to check the valves.

Yes, one of the valves was partially closed due to which the pressure was increasing in the line.

Sandeep opened the valve fully and the pressure showed a gradual decrease and the process began to run smoothly.

Peter thanked him for timely help. He invited them to his home to which both Sandeep and Michael declined.

Sandeep felt relieved as he had solved the problem within two days.

Michael and Katherine appreciated his efforts but that did not satisfy Sandeep because he knew this was not solved by him but by Yutika.

That day again Sandeep went to the same bar but Yutika was not there.

He contacted the owner of the bar and enquired about Yutika.

"She will come late night today." he replied.

Sandeep waited for Yutika to come and she arrived an hour later.

"Hi, I am Sandeep. Remember you gave me an idea regarding the issue of pipeline system?" asked Sandeep.

"Hi, I do remember you. Has the problem been solved?" asked Yutika.

"Yes, it has been solved. I want to thank you for that. You don't know how much you have helped me. This problem if not have been solved, then I could have been fired." said Sandeep.

"It's OK. I have done nothing. It was just a guessing." replied Yutika.

"It might be nothing for you but it worth me more than anything else." said Sandeep.

"By the way, I too want to help you. Can you meet me tomorrow evening at the park?" continued Sandeep.

"May I know why you want to meet me?" asked Yutika.

"Meet me and you will know yourself" said Sandeep and left.

The next day after office hours, Sandeep waited for Yutika at the park.

Yutika came at the appointed time.

"Hello, how are you?" asked Sandeep.

"I am fine. How about you?" she enquired.

"I am fine too." replied Sandeep with a smile.

"I called you here to discuss about your career. I want to know about you. Please." continued Sandeep.

"You want to discuss about my career?" asked Yutika surprisingly.

"Yes, you told me that you have done B.S in Chemical science. If you want then I can help you in getting a job in a multinational company." continued Sandeep.

"It has been years now. I have tried already in many companies but due to one reason or the other, they kept on rejecting me. Now I have stopped applying even for jobs. I am happy working as a bearer in the bar as I have to support my family." said Yutika.

"But do you think your bar career will take you far?" asked Sandeep.

"I have got no other options." said Yutika as tears began rolling down her cheeks.

"Hey, be comfortable. I told you already I am there to help you out. I promise you a job as my secretary. All you need is to assist me in the technical issues." said Sandeep.

"Is it so? Then I prefer to join the job." replied Yutika.

"You may mail me the resume to my maid id." said Sandeep giving her his mail id.

She mailed him her resume and called him to inform the same.

Sandeep took a printout of the resume and began reading it.

Yutika had graduated from a reputed university in USA and her scores were also good. Sandeep could not understand why she did not get a job in her field.

Sandeep forwarded the resume to higher authorities and informed them to arrange for an interview as he needed a person to solve the technical issues.

After a week Sandeep received a mail from the manager mentioning the date on which the interview is to be conducted.

Sandeep told this matter to Yutika and told her to be ready to face an interview.

Yutika started preparing for the interview and started dreaming of a bright career ahead of her.

The day of interview came. Yutika was the alone to be interviewed and she was confident of being getting selected.

The interview began. Sandeep was too present in the interview panel. In the interview Yutika was asked about her family background and slowly the topic was changed to technical round.

She cleared the questions in a single attempt and that too with confidence.

The interview panel was happy with her performance and was asked to wait outside until the panel announces the result.

She waited for the result outside. After ten minutes, Sandeep came out. His face was shining with happiness.

"Congratulations. You have been selected for the job." he said immediately as soon as he saw Yutika.

Yutika could not believe what she heard.

"Are you sure or are you joking?" she asked.

"Why would I joke on a serious issue like this?" mocked Sandeep.

"Also you will be paid $14,000 per month salary." he continued.

He handed the appointment letter to her.

"I am so happy today that I feel like flying in the sky with joy." said Yutika hugging Sandeep.

Sandeep didn't expect this from her but said nothing as he did not want to spoil her happiness.

"I will give you a party tonight. Be present in the HOTEL MILLIONS tonight at 9 pm." she said.

"I will." replied Sandeep with a smile.

This was the first time ever Sandeep has given a smile to a girl in his life. Earlier in his life he could not remember if he had done this before.

The information regarding selection of the new candidate was passed on to others in the company.

Kritika too received a mail regarding the same.

"Hmmm selecting a new candidate and that too an Indian in USA. Let me see Mr. Sandeep how you deal with your work now." she said to herself.

Sandeep arrived a little late at Hotel Millions and saw Yutika sitting at one of the dining table.

She was wearing a red miniskirt with a sleeveless top. She was really looking beautiful that night.

Sandeep came and sat opposite to her.

"Sorry that I am late." he said.

"You are not that much late though." Yutika said with a smile.

"You can order whatever you want. It's my day so every bill will be paid by me." she continued.

Sandeep ordered for an Indian meal and as usual a vegetarian one.

Yutika ordered an Italian food and both of them began to eat their dinner.

After dinner both Sandeep and Yutika left for their homes.

The next day Yutika came to office earlier and waited for Sandeep to come. Sandeep came to the office and greeted her.

After greeting he took her to his cabin and called the peon and told him to tell the other staffs to be ready when they come to get introduced to a new staff who is going to join the company today.

After some talks, both Sandeep and Yutika came out of Sandeep's cabin and he started introducing Yutika to others.

All were happy to meet her except Kritika. She did not introduce herself to Yutika. Sandeep understood why she did this and he introduced Kritika to Yutika.

Sandeep took Yutika to his cabin again and gave her the study materials that she need to go through before understanding the processes the company deals with.

She had good knowledge about chemistry and some basic processes so she did not find it harder to understand the concepts. Also she was a speed learner.

Whenever she had doubts, she would ask Sandeep to clear it and no matter how much Sandeep busy was; he gave his time to Yutika.

Wherever Sandeep went, he took Yutika with her to show her practically how the processes she learnt theoretically worked practically.

Once when returning from the site, Sandeep's car broke down on the way. Yutika too was with him.

"I think it is difficult to get the car repaired at this time." said Sandeep.

"It is very cold here though." replied Yutika.

"Let's go and see if there is any hotel nearby where we could spend the night." said Sandeep and both of them walked towards the city.

After walking for nearly six kilometers, they came across a hotel.

Sandeep went inside the hotel and enquired if they had any rooms any for a night.

"Yes sir, we do have." said the woman at the reception.

"I need two rooms for both of us." continued Sandeep.

The receptionist gave a baffling look at Sandeep as she considered them to be a couple.

"It's OK. Why are you booking two rooms? We can share a single room. After all it is for a night only." said Yutika.

"Are you sure?" asked Sandeep.

"Yes, I am." replied Yutika smiling.

"Then give us a single room please." said Sandeep to the receptionist.

The receptionist smiled and gave him the keys of room number 404.

Both of them went into the room.

The room was big with centrally air conditioned. The yellow lights hanging on the ceiling made the room brighter. On the left side was the bed with two pillows and blankets neatly folded and arranged in a nice manner.

Sandeep closed the door and sat on the bed when his phone rang.

He took the phone and saw the name of the caller. It was Kritika.

"Hello" he said receiving the call.

"Hello, where are you?" she asked.

"I am struck on the way as my car broke down while returning from the site. Any issues?" he enquired after answering her.

"Actually there is a meeting tomorrow morning. President wants to discussion an important issue with us through conference. You need to be present here by 9 am." She said.

"But as far as I know there is no meeting scheduled. Also it is difficult for me to reach office from where I am now." he said again.

"Wherever you may be, you should be present. It is my order." said Kritika all of a sudden changing her way of speaking to Sandeep.

"Your order? What do you mean?" he asked.

"I will tell you. You don't know who I am. Right?" asked Kritika.

"What happened to you?" asked Sandeep not understanding what Kritika was saying to him.

"Yes, I tell you now. I am the daughter of President of this company. Actually you are working under me and not me working under you. All the benefits you got in this company are because of my recommendations and not through your intelligence or your style of working." said Kritika.

"What are you saying? Are you serious?" asked Sandeep again to confirm what she was saying is truth.

"Do you think I am joking at this point of time in the dead night?" shouted Kritika angrily.

"Oh now I see, why Michael and Katherine always supported you whenever I went against you." said Sandeep

"Yes, because they knew who I am and it was me who told you not to tell you." continued Kritika.

Yutika was looking at Sandeep seriously and predicted something serious talk was going on between the caller and Sandeep.

"But why? I want to know why you did this to me. I never asked for this kind of life to you." he said.

"I did this because I loved you from the very first day you came to office. I wanted to marry you and spend my life with you. I knew if you were in India you will not accept me. So I planned and sent you to USA thinking that you will change and accept me as your partner. But here also you did not change. I proposed you on Valentine's Day but you rejected it." Kritika said angrily.

"See, I am too tired now. We will discuss this issue tomorrow morning after the meeting. I need some time." Sandeep told Kritika and disconnected the phone without waiting for her to reply.

"Who was it? And why are you so serious?" asked Yutika after Sandeep kept the phone down.

"It was Kritika." said Sandeep softly.

"What did she say?" enquired Yutika.

"There is a meeting tomorrow and I need to attend it. So need to leave at the morning earlier." replied Sandeep and went off to sleep.

Yutika knew there is something going on between Sandeep and Kritika and he is hiding it from her. She decided not to ask about it until Sandeep himself discloses the matter to her.

The next morning both left early for office after paying the hotel bills.

Sandeep booked a taxi so that they could reach the office on time and soon they were at office.

"Why there is a meeting all of a sudden?" asked Sandeep to Michael.

"Even I don't know. Didn't you see the mail I sent to you? I tried to call you but could not reach you." told Michael.

All of the staffs including Sandeep sat the meeting hall for the meeting to commence. Kritika was the last person to come and sat beside Sandeep.

Sandeep ignored her. Yutika who was standing behind Sandeep saw this and her doubts increased.

The meeting began.

President was on conference call from India. He began.

"As you know, this meeting is called to discuss about the change in company policies which includes the change in working pattern as well. The company management is not satisfied with the employees who have been non performers for the past one year and we have come with a decision for them." he said.

All were confused as to why President began with the issue of non performers.

"Mr. Sandeep, let's begin from you." continued President.

"Yes sir." Sandeep replied.

"The management is satisfied with your performance but has observed that you have got to hide something from the organization. May be that is personal but still you do not feel normal when it comes to personal issues. Why is it so?" asked the President.

"It is nothing of that kind sir. I believe that personal issues should be kept away from the professional issues." he replied.

In this way the meeting continued for an hour and when all were about to leave, Mr. President asked Sandeep to wait for few more minutes as he had some other issues to discuss with him.

Once every one left, the President again continued.

"See, I have something to discuss with you and that is personal. You know whatever you are today is because of my daughter?" asked the President.

"Sir, I tell you frankly. I used to believe that all these promotions and the trip to USA was due to the recognition of my intelligence rather than the influence of your daughter." said Sandeep.

"See, until now there is nothing that I have not provided her. I have given her whatever she has asked for and this time too I wish to do the same." said the President.

"Sir, that is your personal issue. Why are you saying me that?" asked Sandeep surprised.

"I am saying you this because this time she has asked for something that cannot be given to her without the consent." said the President.

"What is that sir?" enquired Sandeep.

"This time she is asking for you. She wants to marry you and spend her life with you." continued the President.

Sandeep sat silent for a moment and thinking for a moment he spoke, "Sir, you don't know about my family background. I come from a middle class family. For me my parents are everything. There is nothing beyond them. As far as your daughter is concerned, she proposed me recently during the Valentine's Day but I rejected her proposal because I know I am not the right person for her."

"But what's wrong in accepting her?" asked the President again.

"Sir, please I don't want to discuss this issue any more. I am not made for her." replied Sandeep and left the meeting room.

The next day Yutika was working on her table and Sandeep has not yet arrived. Michael came to office a little earlier.

"Good morning, Yutika" he said.

"Good morning Michael. Do you know when Sandeep will come?" asked Yutika.

"Actually, actually,……" Michael kept silent.

"Actually, what?" asked Yutika.

"Actually, he has met with an accident yesterday night and is in a critical condition at hospital." said Michael.

"What?" asked Yutika with a shock.

"Why didn't anyone tell me of this?" she continued.

"I met him today morning at the hospital but the doctors say nothing can be said." said Michael.

Yutika took her phone and tried to call him but his phone was not reachable.

She grew more miserable as she did not what to do now. She kept on trying to call Sandeep again and again but his phone was still not reachable.

She closed her eyes and prayed to God and began to leave the office to see Sandeep. Just then the door opened. It was Sandeep.

All of a sudden she ran towards him and hug him and started crying.

"You here?" asked Yutika in a surprise.

"What do you mean?" asked Sandeep.

"Michael told me that you have met with an accident yesterday night and also you are in a critical condition." she continued.

"What the fuck!" shouted Sandeep.

He summoned Michael and demanded an explanation.

"Hey man cool. Today is All Fool's Day. I just played a prank on her. Nothing else." replied Michael.

THAP… Sandeep slapped Michael.

The whole office was watching this.

"Is this the manner in which you play pranks on your colleagues? Don't you have any sense?" shouted Sandeep.

Michael was silent as he felt embarrassed.

"Apologize to Yutika for your cheap behavior." said Sandeep.

Michael simply stared at Sandeep and Yutika without saying anything.

"It's ok. No need to apologize." said Yutika and pulled Sandeep back.

All of them resumed to their work. Sandeep and Yutika went to Sandeep's cabin.

Kritika came and knocked the door of Sandeep's cabin.

"Yes, come in." said Sandeep.

Kritika came in. Seeing her Sandeep stood up from his seat.

"Why are you standing up?" asked Kritika.

"For me you are daughter of President of this company. You should at least receive this much respect." said Sandeep.

"Sandeep, are you mad? I have come to ask you if you were right in behaving yourself with Michael?" she asked.

"You know what he did. I don't think I have done anything wrong." replied Sandeep.

"You should have talked to him personally rather than embarrassing him in the public." said Kritika.

"I know what I am doing. You need not advice me." said Sandeep in a stern voice.

That night Sandeep received a message from Kritika asking him to meet her at Hotel Millions.

Sandeep informed this to Yutika and told her to accompany him.

"Why should I come?" asked Yutika.

"I don't want to meet Kritika alone. She will discuss useless issues which I don't want to discuss at all. May be in your presence she will not do so." said Sandeep.

"But maybe there is something she wants to discuss really important this time." said Yutika.

"Whatever it may be. You are coming. That's it." said Sandeep and insisted Yutika to come with him.

She finally accepted the invitation and went along with Sandeep.

They reached Hotel Millions at the appointed time and saw Kritika waiting for Sandeep.

"Don't worry. If there is anything I will talk to her." said Sandeep

Both of them went and sat opposite to Kritika.

"You? Who told you to come?" asked Kritika angrily at Yutika.

Yutika looked at Sandeep as if asking what she should do.

"Be cool Kritika. What happened to you?" asked Sandeep.

"I just wanted to meet you and not Yutika. Who told you to bring her with you?" asked Kritika.

"Sandeep, we will meet tomorrow at the office. I have to go now." Yutika said and left the place without waiting for Sandeep to say anything.

"Yutika, wait. Where are you going?" asked Sandeep but Yutika was already gone.

"Kritika, what's all this? What's your problem with Yutika?" asked

"Look I am telling you that I want to spend my life with you. Why don't you understand that?" asked Kritika directly.

"See, I am not here for romancing. I am just here for my career. I tell you that if required I will resign my job and go elsewhere but the only reason why I am not going is...." said Sandeep and stopped in between.

"Tell me the reason." demanded Kritika.

"Nothing. Leave it." said Sandeep.

"I tell you the reason. You are not leaving because of Yutika. Am I right?" asked Kritika.

"What do you want to say?" asked Sandeep again.

"The truth is you love her and it is because of her you are not accepting me. Is it because she is more intelligent than me or she is more beautiful than me?" shouted Kritika.

"I don't know how to tell you but be it either you or her; I don't want either of you. I am just guiding her in her career. She has the capability to go ahead of me if she performs in this manner." said Sandeep.

"You are guiding her in her career by making her sit with you all day long. You call it guidance?" shouted Kritika again.

"I tell you directly now. There is nothing between Yutika and me. We are just friends and nothing beyond that." saying this Sandeep left the place.

Yutika who left earlier from the hotel began to doubt Kritika as to why she not wanted her presence.

May be she thought Kritika has got in a relationship with Sandeep and Sandeep is hiding it from her.

It was the month of June and on 3rd June, it was Yutika's birthday.

"Sandeep, I want to tell you something." said Yutika.

"Tell me. I am there for you always." said Sandeep.

"Tomorrow is my birthday." said Yutika.

"Is it? Let's celebrate it then." said Sandeep.

"Oh sure. I will give you a party tomorrow night." said Yutika with a smile.

"No, this time though it is your birthday, I will give the party for you. You will just attend it." said Sandeep.

"Ok anyway. I am so happy for that." replied Yutika with a smile.

It was the most beautiful smile Sandeep has ever seen. He tried to ignore that smile but could not. His eyes were looking at her beautiful smile. He didn't know what happened to him all of a sudden.

Sandeep planned a surprise for her. He ordered for a cake for her birthday with her name mentioned.

Sandeep mailed to the staffs informing them of Yutika's birthday. When he opened his mail, he saw there was a mail from Kritika.

Sandeep opened the mail which read:

Dear Sandeep,

Despite me telling you that I want to spend my life with you, you are avoiding me directly nowadays. I can expel you from the company within moments. But I won't do that because I hope someday or the other you will understand me and come to me and accept me to be your wife.

If you think there are any financial differences between us, then I tell you that you can stay at my home after our marriage. I can give you all that you want. But please do accept me. In case you don't accept me, I will not leave you forever in your life.

With regards,
KRITIKA

Sandeep grew furious and decided to submit his resignation to the President.

He wrote a mail to the President which read:

Respected Sir,

You already know what is going on between your daughter and me. I am not such kind of person who is in this company for romancing a girl. I tell you again that I am not the suitable boy for your girl in terms of your status and financial status.

I accept your daughter has got talent as well as beauty but how is it possible to marry a girl whom you just don't love at all? I request you to talk to your daughter regarding this issue and I want to conclude this issue here only with any further talks on the same.

Thanking you,
Sandeep

The next day Yutika came to the office a little before time.

She was wearing a pink miniskirt with white shirt and a pink overcoat. Her eyes were shining as her eyes were eyelashed. Her lips shone with lipsticks. She was the glamour girl of the day. Everybody kept watching her and could not remove their eyes from her. Such was her beauty on that day.

She entered Sandeep's cabin. Sandeep who was busy with his work did not notice Yutika coming in.

"Hello." said Yutika.

Sandeep saw her lifting his head up. He could not believe what he saw. He never expected Yutika to be so beautiful as he is seeing her today.

"Beautiful" were the words that first came from his mouth in an unconscious manner.

"How am I looking today?" asked Yutika.

Sandeep has never before told any girl of how beautiful she looks but now a girl is asking him of her own.

"Well, you look really beautiful. Wish you a many more happy returns of the day." said Sandeep.

"Oh thank you so much." said Yutika giving Sandeep a hug.

When she hugged Sandeep, he could smell the fragrance of the scent she has applied and that was intoxicating.

"Come to the Hotel Millions. I have arranged the party there." said Sandeep.

"You know Sandeep, I am so happy today that I cannot express my happiness to you. Really it totally feels different to spend the time with you." said Yutika.

That evening all the staffs gathered at hotel millions. The hotel's hall was well decorated with flowers on the walls. The music that was going on at the background was melodious. There were different drinks and snacks.

The cake was brought to the center of the hall. Yutika stood with a knife in her hand and started cutting the cake while the staffs sang the happy birthday song.

She cut the first piece of the cake and gave it to Sandeep. Sandeep took a little bit and passed the remaining to Yutika.

Kritika who was watching all this grew more furious this time. Yet she remained patient trying not to create ruckus in the party.

Everybody now gave their presents to Yutika and wished her too. Kritika was the last one to wish her. She had not brought any gifts to Yutika.

"Don't be too happy because this happiness is not going to last longer." she said.

Yutika could not understand what Kritika said.

Sandeep who was with Yutika pulled Kritika aside.

"Why don't you behave properly at least in the party? It is her birthday today. Atleast let her celebrate." said Sandeep.

"You are saying as if I have stopped her from celebrating. See, the celebration is going on already. After all it is the party thrown by Mr. Sandeep." said Kritika angrily.

The party went till late night. After 11 pm one by one left for home. Yutika and Sandeep were the last one to leave.

Both sat in Sandeep's car.

"Yutika, I will leave you at your home." said Sandeep.

"It is already late now. Would you mind if I stayed with you for a night?" asked Yutika.

Sandeep saw Yutika for a moment. He did not prefer her staying with him but on the other side he don't want her to feel miserable.

"Ok. You may stay at my home tonight." said Sandeep and drove the car towards his home.

Once they reached Sandeep's home, Yutika went into the kitchen and started preparing tea.

"Why are you preparing tea now at this dead night?" asked Sandeep.

"I want to talk to you something. I want you to listen it patiently." said Yutika.

Both had their tea and were sitting on the couch.

Yutika began.

"I don't know what is going on between Kritika and you and neither I do wish to know about it." said Yutika.

"Why are you so serious always with Kritika? Try to check why she is like that. May be she has her own problems." she said looking at Sandeep.

"You don't know about Kritika. She being the daughter of President is controlling the company and me like the way she wants it to be. I am not going to let that happen at any cost." replied Sandeep.

"Sandeep, in fact I too feel the same toward you. I mean I too have feelings for you." Yutika said and saw at Sandeep but he has already slept.

Yutika too slept and both went to office together the next morning.

Sandeep wanted to go to India as it had been long time he has spent in USA. He applied for leave of one month and that was granted to him.

He booked his tickets to Ahmedabad for the next week and called him mother to inform her about his coming.

"Hello mom, I am coming to Ahmedabad next week." said Sandeep.

His mother was too happy to hear this and started preparing his favorite dishes to serve him.

Sandeep informed about his going to India to Yutika and she felt a little sad about it.

"Will you not come back?" she asked.

"I don't think so I should come back other than required. I have asked for transfer to India back." he said smiling.

"I will really miss you a lot." said Yutika trying to hide her tears.

"Can we have dinner together? Who knows whether we will have parties and dinners together or not in the future?" she said in a sad voice.

"Of course, we will have." replied Sandeep with a smile. He was happy and was counting days to return to India.

Both of them used to go to shopping together almost daily during the evenings.

Sandeep would buy things for Yutika whatever she asked him to buy. He gifted her diamond ring and a golden pendant chain.

As the days went, Yutika turned more miserable.

"What's the matter with you? Why do you look sad?" asked Sandeep one day.

"Nothing. I am as usual and normal." replied Yutika but Sandeep could understand that she was lying.

"See, you cannot lie to me. I can clearly see it on your face." said Sandeep again to know what has happened to Yutika.

"Sandeep, I feel sad about missing you. I cannot think myself to be alone without you." said Yutika and started crying.

"Is this the issue after all? We can be in touch through emails and phone calls. I will call you regularly even though I will be India." said Sandeep.

It was a different feeling for Yutika. She wanted to confess her love to Sandeep but she couldn't make the move.

She thought of various ways of saying it to Sandeep by writing an email or sometimes by speaking to him directly but whenever she saw him, she feared about losing his friendship if she tells him the truth.

She decided to write a letter to him telling him about her love.

Dear Sandeep,

I know you will never come back to USA once you are settled in India. I am not saying that is wrong as your parents too live in India.

The help you have done to me is not smaller. You have ignited a new life in me. It's because of you that I am in this organization and having a job. Else I would have been a waitress in the bar.

Whenever you are around, I feel an unknown courage within me which helps me in speaking to the people even who are unknown to me.

Sandeep, I don't know whether you have seen through my eyes or not but I have started loving you. I have tried to say it to you many times but somehow I could not say it.

Hope after reading this letter, you will accept me.

Always yours,
Yutika.

She wrote this letter and put it in his bag.

It was the final evening Sandeep was going to spend in USA. He called all his office staffs for a dinner and offered them a party. All the staffs gave their best wishes to him.

Sandeep's flight was at afternoon at 1 pm the next day. Yutika came along with him to the airport to drop him off.

"Sandeep, are you sure you need to go back?" asked Yutika once again.

Sandeep kept his hands on her jaws and said, "See, I need to go. I came here just for a project and that is completed now. So I need to be back. You have your career ahead. You need to focus on it without my support anymore. Life is not that much easy as you think it to be. There was a time when you needed me but it is the time now that you should support yourself in my absence and I know you can do that."

"I will not be able to do in your absence. It is your presence that makes me work like anything." said Yutika trying to hide her tears.

"There's nothing like that. I know you can do it." said Sandeep when his name was announced for check in.

"It's time to say bye. Take care." saying this Sandeep left.

Yutika stood back alone and saw Sandeep going through the security checks.

She could now feel the absence of him. It was for her as if she was left alone in an unknown place with unknown people.

Sandeep sat on his seat in the flight and put on his seat belt. He too felt different this time as if he has left something back in USA. He tried to sleep but the thought of Yutika kept haunting him.

Yutika decided not to go to office that day but instead went to Sandeep's home. She opened the door and went in.

She went to his room and closed the door and started crying loudly.

"Sandeep, you should not have done this to me. You should have taken me with you to India but you didn't and neither had you informed me earlier." she yelled while crying and after sometime she slept in the room itself.

After flying for nearly twenty two hours he landed at Ahmedabad and went to his home.

He was given a warm welcome by his parents. He spoke to them about his experiences in USA and after talking for some time, went to have a bath.

His mother was cleaning his room and she transferred the bags to his room when a piece of paper fell on the floor.

She picked it up and opened it. She could not understand what was written as it was written in English.

When Sandeep came after having a bath, she told him that she got this piece of paper from one of his bags and handed it over to him.

Sandeep opened the paper to read what it was. It was the letter from Yutika mentioning her feelings for him.

"What is written in it?" asked his mom.

"Nothing mom." replied Sandeep and kept the letter in one of his books.

He called Yutika in the afternoon.

"Hi, have you reached India safely?" was the first question Yutika asked Sandeep on receiving the call.

"Yes, I did. I wanted to ask you one thing." said Sandeep.

"Yes?" asked Yutika.

"Did you put any letter in my bag?" asked Sandeep.

"Well, did you read it? I hope you are not angry with me after reading it." replied Yutika.

"Yutika, you know I will not return to USA and at this point you have handed me this letter. I don't believe in all these love stuffs. I have just helped you to start your career and I have seen that you have progressed well. In fact, I am expecting a day when I will be working under you and you will be my boss." said Sandeep.

"But career is different than life. Both should go hand in hand." said Yutika.

"I tell you that if you have career others will come to you on their own. There are better persons than me who can care for you well. I don't think I am the right person in your life." said Sandeep trying to distract her.

"Sandeep, I really miss you and I expect you to be in USA soon." said Yutika and the phone got disconnected.

Both Sandeep and Yutika used to talk for hours sometimes on the phone and send mails to each other but everything was official and there was nothing personal between them.

One day Yutika called Sandeep.

"You know I have got a promotion." she said cheeringly.

"Congrats. I knew this is going to happen soon." said Sandeep.

"Now I have six trainees working under me and they need to be taught about the process control and others." Yutika said.

"Well then you are a team leader now." told Sandeep smiling.

"Of course, I am. But you know all these trainees are new and some of them don't know even the basics." she said.

"Don't worry. They will learn and may even become expert as you are their teacher now." joked Sandeep.

"Shut up. I am telling it seriously." said Yutika.

"Is there any new project scheduled?" asked Sandeep.

"Yes, they have handed me a document related to new project. This project I am planning to teach to my trainees as well. They will get better idea once they see it practically." said Yutika.

"Well, if you have any problem then feel free to contact me anytime. I am ready to help you." said Sandeep.

"Did Sandeep contact you?" asked Kritika to Yutika.

"Yes, in fact we talk with each other almost daily." said Yutika.

"He used to ignore me and now seems to be attracted towards you. I warn you to be away from him. He is mine and never can be yours. Remember that." said Kritika to Yutika who was listening to their conversation a little before.

"But I never said anything to him." said Yutika again.

"Never ever think of talking to him again. I warn you or else you will be expelled from the company." shouted Kritika.

Kritika wrote an email to Sandeep warning him of the consequences he will be facing in case he ignored Kritika again and should accept her at any cost.

For Sandeep this was too much and he felt more frustrated now because of Kritika.

On the same night Sandeep received a call. It was from Yutika.

"Hello, did you receive any mail from Kritika?" she asked.

"Yes I did but don't worry. She won't do what she says. She is just threatening us and nothing more." said Sandeep just to console Yutika but he knew Kritika would go to any extent to achieve him.

Yutika took her students to the project site and taught them about the basics of the installation like the way Sandeep used to teach her.

The installation was going on well until a problem rose.

The pressure in the pipeline was getting increased each time Yutika tried to increase the temperature.

Not knowing what to do, she contacted Sandeep.

"Hello, Sandeep, I am facing a technical problem here. I need your help." said Yutika.

"What's it?" asked Sandeep.

"The pressure is getting increased on its own whenever I try to increase the temperature even a little higher. I do not know what to do." said Yutika.

"Cool. Arrange the students first in a sequence on the control panel. I will handle it from here." he said.

Yutika did as was told to her by Sandeep.

Sandeep began controlling the process through phone from India and it was going smoothly.

"I want one of you to go and check the valve." said Sandeep.

"I am going Sandeep." said Yutika.

"No, not you. Let one of the student go." insisted Sandeep.

"They might not know where the control valve is located. I need to do it." replied Yutika and headed towards the valve.

She also took her phone with her for discussion with Sandeep.

"Be careful while checking the valve. Anything can happen anytime." warned Sandeep.

All of the sudden there was a noise as if someone has fallen down on the lane.

"Hello, hello, Yutika?" shouted Sandeep on the phone. But there was no response.

"Hello, you there?" again shouted Sandeep.

But still there was no response.

"Please reply something. I want to know what is going on over there. Yutika, reply. What happened to you?" shouted Sandeep again as he doubted something has went wrong with Yutika.

After sometime a voice on the phone spoke.

"Hello sir." said the voice.

"Hello, who's this?" asked Sandeep.

"Sir, I am George. I am one of the trainees working under Yutika madam." came the reply.

"What happened to her? Why is she not speaking?" asked Sandeep curiously.

"Actually sir……" there was a deep silence.

"Actually what? Tell me." shouted Sandeep.

"Actually, Yutika madam slipped and fell in the nitrogen tank located nearby. She is being rescued now. She is in a semi conscious state." told George.

"What? How? I mean how did she slip off? Did anyone rescue her?" came one after the other questions from Sandeep.

"Yes sir, she has been rescued and they are taking her to the hospital. We are waiting for an ambulance to come." said George.

"Ok. You keep the phone on her ears. I will speak to her." said Sandeep.

"But sir, she is not in a position to speak now." said George again.

"Do as I say. Don't argue." said Sandeep as he lost his temper.

George did as was told by Sandeep.

George kept the phone of Yutika's ears and told Sandeep to speak to her.

"Hello, Yutika. See, I am there with you. Don't worry. Everything will be alright. Just be cool. God is there with you. You will be back soon." said Sandeep in a single breath.

But there was no reply from Yutika. She was losing her consciousness but could hear Sandeep's voice which gave her more courage to come out of the trauma.

After a while George spoke again, "Sir, Yutika madam has been taken to the hospital in an ambulance."

"Ok. Is she suffering seriously?" asked Sandeep to confirm.

Though it was a serious issue, George declined to tell Sandeep and told him that there is nothing serious and she will be fine.

Sandeep could not trust George. So he called the Ahmedabad airport and booked a ticket for himself to Illinois.

"Mom, I am going back to USA for a week." said Sandeep.

"But you have just come. Why do you want to go early?" asked his mom.

"But it is a serious issue. You won't understand. I need to go but I promise I will be back soon." said Sandeep and began packing his bag.

He mailed to the staffs about an urgent meeting that needs to be discussed immediately regarding to Yutika's issue and he fixed the time at night as per IST.

All the staffs were present at the meeting including Kritika.

He put the meeting on the conference call so that it could be an open discussion instead of individual discussion.

"I have called this meeting with regard to whatever has happened to Yutika today morning." Sandeep began.

"I would like to know why was there any senior experience personnel not present on the site from our company and only trainees were allowed with her." he continued.

"Good question Mr. Sandeep Mishra." said Kritika clapping her hands.

"I would like to remind you that you have trained her how to deal with the installation and other issues. Also she had trainees with her this time. Do you think she undertook the trainees without knowing how to face an emergency in the workplace?" asked Kritika.

"This is not the answer to my question. Even though there were trainees, her experience is not enough to deal with the emergency situations that arose today. She is intelligent, I accept but sometimes even an intelligent person commits mistakes." said Sandeep calmly.

"Whom do you want to blame? Tell it directly instead of beating around the bush." shouted back Kritika.

Everyone in the meeting was surprised as to why was Kritika shouting like this and that too during the meeting.

"See Kritika, I am not blaming anyone. I am just telling that she could have been accompanied by any other staffs instead of just the trainees." said Sandeep again.

"You are saying this because you have got feelings for her. You simply love her. You don't want her to get affected." said Kritika as if blaming Sandeep.

"Remember it is you who brought her to the company and you made her your technical assistant for solving your technical issues. Why did you bring her first?" asked Kritika.

Sandeep was silent for a moment.

"OK. I am responsible for all these things. I accept. Happy now?" he asked.

There was no reply from Kritika and the meeting was ended.

Sandeep took the flight and was on the way to Illinois.

He could not wait to see Yutika's condition. Even the air hostess's smile failed to bring a smile on his face.

He smiled back just for the sake of smiling. Each time he closed his eyes to sleep, the image of Yutika smiling would come to his mind.

He landed at the airport by the evening. He already had informed Michael about his arrival and Michael was there to receive him at the airport.

"Michael, what is the present condition of Yutika?" asked Sandeep immediately on seeing Michael.

Michael was silent and did not reply anything.

"Michael, I am asking you something if you can hear me." said Sandeep as he was losing his temper now.

"Do you want to go to hospital directly or have your dinner first?" asked Michael trying to evade the question.

"Let's go to the hospital. I need to see Yutika as soon as possible." said Sandeep.

They reached the hospital. It was a private hospital and every treatment facilities were available in this hospital. The smell of the hospital was so stinking that Sandeep could not bear it.

Both went to the receptionist where a lady was sitting at the desk.

"Madam, we want to meet Ms. Yutika who has been admitted here. May we know in which ward she has been admitted?" said Michael.

"Go to the third floor and take right. She has been admitted in the I.C.U." replied the receptionist.

"Is she so serious that she is admitted in I.C.U?" asked Sandeep pulling Michael back who was walking ahead of him.

"Yes, we have not said her true condition. She has not regained her consciousness for the last four days. Even the doctors don't understand why it is so. A doctor from France is coming to treat her. We are waiting for him to come." said Michael in a low voice.

Sandeep stood still where he was standing. He felt dizziness and his body went cold.

"Sandeep, Sandeep, are you ok?" asked Michael who held Sandeep now with his hands to prevent him from falling unconscious.

"I am fine. Let's go." said Sandeep and started walking towards the third floor. They took the right turn and a board read I.C.U in bold letters.

Sandeep had not the courage to see Yutika in I.C.U so he stood at a distance from the I.C.U.

"What happened? Come with me. Let's go in." insisted Michael.

"No, I can't see Yutika in this condition." pleaded Sandeep.

"But you need to see her. May be on seeing you she will regain her consciousness." said Michael.

Sandeep opened the door and saw Yutika from a distance.

Yutika lay still on the bed with tubes running from the ventilator to her nose. Some tubes were pinched in her hands. She was covered with blanket from legs to her neck.

Sandeep closed his eyes and tears began to roll from his eyes. He could not control it. This was the first time Michael saw Sandeep in a gloomy mood. Sandeep had been cheerful always but this time he could not even give a smile to the hospital staffs.

Sandeep slowly walked towards Yutika and saw her closely. He held her palms on his hand.

"Yutika, I have come back. See, I am speaking to you." said Sandeep. But there was no response from Yutika.

"You need to gain consciousness at least for me. You cannot leave this world. You have got many more to do. You cannot leave your duties in between. Who will train the trainees who are working under you if you leave?" said Sandeep crying continuously.

"I know anyhow you will regain your consciousness and be back with more energy than ever. The doctors are doubtful about you because they don't think you will regain conscious. I know my Yutika better than what they know. Please for me you need to regain your consciousness." said Sandeep and started crying more profusely.

Michael came from behind and lifted Sandeep.

"Come, let's go. The visitor's time is over Sandeep." saying this he dragged Sandeep outside I.C.U.

They went to the hotel. Sandeep didn't want to eat anything but Michael pressurized him to have something and Sandeep ate too little just for the sake of eating.

Sandeep went to his home and opened the door. He could not believe his eyes. Everything has changed. His home is being kept cleaner than ever. He didn't know who did it. He went around his home and saw Yutika's belongings at his home. He understood that she had been living in his home on his absence.

On the table he found a diary which had a pen inside it. Sandeep hesitated whether to read it or not. But out of curiosity he opened the diary.

It was Yutika's diary. He opened the first page where she has written her introduction.

He turned to the next page and there was a title mentioned FROM WAITRESS TO ENGINEER.

He began reading it. Yutika had mentioned about how she joined the company with the help of Sandeep and how her life was when she was working as a waitress in a pub.

One of the paragraphs attracted Sandeep's eyes which read:

It was the day when Sandeep first came to the bar. He did not drink though. I saw from distance and recognized him to be an Indian. So I didn't ask him if he wanted to drink thinking that he may feel bad.

Sandeep and his friend were discussing a technical problem of which I have already studied during my college days and I suggested my own idea to them which was later applied by Sandeep and he succeeded. He came back to meet me and asked about my qualification and promised me a job in his company. At first I didn't believe him but when he asked for my resume I began to trust him and somehow I don't know whether it was just the trust or I was falling in love with him.

One thing I like about Sandeep is that he always used to maintain distance between him and me while interacting; the one which is common among Indians. Earlier I used to hate men because while working as a waitress there has been times when I had been abused by the customers but I was helpless. But Sandeep knew always how to respect and treat a girl more than her expectation.

I hope someday or the other the distance between Sandeep and me will decrease and he will be with me always forever.

Just as Sandeep was reading this he heard footsteps from behind. He turned back to see who it was. Kritika was standing at the hall.

"Why have you come here?" asked Sandeep.

"When you have come from India to meet Yutika, can't I come here?" asked Kritika.

"But I have got nothing to do with you. I don't want to see you at all. Please leave from here." shouted Sandeep.

Kritika was drunk and Sandeep got to know about this as she came near him.

"Have you drunk?" asked Sandeep.

"Yes, I have Mr. Sandeep. What did you think that I am not a drinker? You are a fool." said Kritika and started laughing madly.

"What do you want now from me?" asked Sandeep.

"Nothing. I have just asked one thing from you and that is just you. Nothing more than that." replied Kritika.

"What if I don't do that?" asked Sandeep.

"Yutika and you both will face the consequences through me." said Kritika and again started laughing.

"You will not do anything like that. I plead you to leave me. I am not the right person for you." said Sandeep as a last effort.

"No, never. I mean what I said." shouted Kritika.

"Can we postpone the discussion of issue until Yutika recovers?" asked Sandeep.

"Yes, I can wait for you even for years. Yutika's recovery is just days away." said Kritika and left Sandeep's home.

The next day Sandeep again with Michael visited the hospital. He had Yutika's diary with him in his hand.

"What is that you are holding?" asked Michael.

Sandeep opened the diary and showed him the paragraph where Yutika had written about Sandeep.

He also told Michael about Kritika's visit to his home.

Sandeep's name was announced from the I.C.U. to visit Yutika. Sandeep went inside and sat beside Yutika. She had been laying in the same condition as she was when he came yesterday.

"Has the doctor from France arrived?" asked Sandeep to the nurse who was in charge of the I.C.U.

"Yes, he is at present going through the medical reports and will be treating her soon." she replied.

Sandeep asked for the doctor's name and went to meet him. He wanted to meet him personally for which the permission was granted by the authorities in the hospital.

"See doctor, I want her to be totally cured. I don't know why she is unconscious for all these days. I don't mind how much the expense will be I am ready to pay but all i need is her speedy recovery." said Sandeep.

"Don't worry Mr. Sandeep. We are trying our best." said the doctor.

Sandeep became unhappy on hearing this and went again inside the I.C.U. He held her hands again and spoke to Yutika.

"See, I have spoken to the doctor who has come from France to treat you. He has assured me of your recovery." said Sandeep.

As he said this sentence, he began to cry again. Tears began to fall on Yutika's hand wetting her hand.

Yutika's hand began to move slowly. She started moving her fingers.

Sandeep gave a look at Yutika to check if what he was experiencing was true and indeed it was. She was slowly opening her eyes now. Sandeep went out and came along with the doctor.

The doctor checked her and said that she was normal but still some tests need to be taken to confirm it and if everything was fine she may be soon discharged.

The doctor came and was surprised to see Yutika awake.

"This is a miracle in medical science," he told Sandeep.

Sandeep was too happy and tears of joy flowed through his eyes. He held again Yutika's hands and said, "You don't know how much happy I am."

Yutika could not speak but just whispered Sandeep's name again and again.

"It's ok. You are fine now. Keep calm." said Sandeep.

While all this was going on, Kritika and Michael came and stood behind Sandeep.

"Very good Mr. Sandeep." said Kritika clapping her hands. "You have got to do some discussion and take a decision soon if you remember." she said reminding of what Sandeep had told her last night.

"Yes, I am going to take the decision soon that will benefit everyone including me." replied Sandeep.

It was not before two days that Yutika was discharged from the hospital. Sandeep used to feed her food and used to take care of her for day and night. Sometimes he even went sleepless. He did not know even why he is doing all this. Whatever he was doing on the back of his mind he was always remembering that he had to give a full stop to what was going on between Kritika, Yutika and him.

Yutika was now feeling better and she used to do the rituals on her own.

"Sandeep, I am planning to go to office tomorrow." she said.

"Are you sure about that?" asked Sandeep.

"Yes, I am better than before now. I feel I am perfectly alright now." she said with a smile.

"Are you going to stay in USA permanently now?" she asked to Sandeep.

"Yes, I am going to reside here forever. I have no plans to go to India." replied Sandeep.

"You know I am so happy to hear that you are here after all." said Yutika winking at Sandeep.

Sandeep said nothing and got lost in his thoughts.

The next day Yutika left for office. Sandeep was at home cooking the lunch for her.

After Yutika left, Sandeep went to the medical store nearby and brought a syringe.

He came home and wrote an email to both Kritika and Yutika with the subject THE CONFESSION.

Dear Kritika,

The time has come to take the final decision on the issues going on amongst us. The moment you are reading this letter, I may be not there to read the reply that I may be receiving from you.

I tried to explain you that I am not the right person of your life but you could not understand it. I tried to say it through kindness as well as angrily but all that emotions had no effect on you.

I told you the decision I will be making will benefit all the three of us. You may call me coward or courageous person, I don't mind. This is my last letter to you as I am leaving this world forever.

Thanking you,

SANDEEP

Next he wrote a letter to Yutika which read:

Dear Yutika,

I came to know through your diary that you are in love with me. But I tell you that I am not the right person with whom you should fall in love with. I have supported you at all critical times as you did to me once when I was facing the technical problem in the company.

I tell you that this may not be possible in the future. I mean I cannot be always present with you for supporting you for the rest of your life. I want you to move ahead with your life lonely and succeed in it.

When the right time comes, do get married but do not name your children Sandeep as I don't want to haunt you even in your memories.

You have not yet seen the open world. Live your life the way you want rather than living it for somebody else. I always wanted to see you happy but I tell until I am there you cannot progress ahead in your life.

I have only one last wish to make. When you see me next time, be sure you don't cry because I don't want you to be miserable for me.

Thanking you,

SANDEEP.

He mailed the letter to both Kritika and Yutika.

After mailing he took the injection and prayed to the God one last time because he knew there is going to be an end somehow.

He pinched the injected in his nerves and injected the air inside the nerve. After half an hour, he could feel dizziness. His eyes started closing and he was feeling unconscious. Sweat began to flow from his forehead and his chest began to pain. His room which was bright a little before was now turning into darkness. He was starting to suffer from a heart attack.

He smiled for the last time and lay on the floor and closed his eyes forever.

Yutika opened her mail and the only mail in her inbox was from Sandeep.

She opened it and after reading she felt the shock like never before. She called Kritika and told her about the mail.

Kritika too checked her mail and read the mail that she had received from Sandeep.

Both Yutika and Kritika came to Sandeep's home together. The entrance door was locked. They broke open the door and entered in.

"Sandeep, where are you?" shouted Yutika and Kritika. But there was no reply.

Both began to search for Sandeep in the whole house and found him in his bedroom.

He was lying still without any movement with his eyes closed.

"Sandeep, wake up." shouted Yutika holding Sandeep's hands. She felt how cold his hand was. She started rubbing his hands but he showed no movement. Yutika saw the injection lying beside him but there were no any medicines to be found nearby. Yutika understood that he had committed suicide with the help of this injection. But how did he do that was the question.

Kritika called an ambulance and they took him to the hospital. The doctors took him to the emergency ward and began the treatment on him. But he did not respond to the treatment as it was already too late.

The doctor came out after some time.

"Doctor, what happened to him?" asked Yutika almost crying.

"I am sorry. He is already dead. He has suffered from a heart attack." replied the doctor and went away.

The world came to a standstill for Yutika. She wanted to cry madly but she remembered Sandeep's last mail reminding her of not to cry for him.

"How do you say that he suffered from a heart attack? He had neither the habit of smoking nor of drinking." intervened Kritika.

"See, do you see this small hole in his hand?" asked the doctor showing Sandeep's hand.

Both Kritika and Yutika nodded.

"That's the point to note." continued the doctor.

"He had committed suicide by injecting the injection inside the nerves." said the doctor.

"But how could that lead to death?" asked Kritika. "There were no medicines beside him." she continued.

"He has injected nothing but just an air inside the nerves. When air is injected inside the nerves, air bubbles are formed inside the nerves which get enlarged as the time progresses. This enlargement of air bubbles blocks the oxygen that passes through them and this affects the heart which leads to heart attack within half an hour." said the doctor.

The news of his death was sent to the company and a funeral process was arranged for him.

Moments before Sandeep was to be cremated, Yutika went near him and began kissing him because she knew this was her last chance of seeing Sandeep and he would be gone forever.

He was cremated in the graveyard of the nearby church. After the cremation was over, all went except Kritika and Yutika.

They stood there for one more hour and both of them went back.

Yutika came to Sandeep's home. This time she felt differently when she entered the home. She could not rejoice her home coming.

Tears were already choking her throat. She drank two glasses of water and went to the place where Sandeep lay dead a day before.

She had a picture of Sandeep which she had once taken while during one of the talks she had with him and he was smiling in that picture.

She enlarged the picture in her laptop and took a print out of it and framed it and hanged it on the wall.

"Sandeep, I could feel your presence at least through your photograph. You smile is there to motivate me during my hard times." she said and started crying uncontrollably.

She also took one more copy of the photograph and hanged in her cabin where she used to sit beside Sandeep.

Whenever Yutika used to go for shopping or to places where she had visited along with Sandeep, she would be reminded of him and she would sometimes feel miserable. Days and months passed by and she slowly came out of her miserable condition and started living a normal life.

ONE YEAR LATER

"You know Sandeep, I have got promotion but I have declined the offer because if I accept it, my location as well as my cabin would be changed. I don't want to leave your cabin. Even today your seat remains vacant. Nobody can replace your post. I want the life to be the same as it was during your presence." said Yutika looking at Sandeep's photo at her home.

Years passed by and everything now turned normal in everyone's life. Kritika is now President of the company. Yutika now deals with the issues all by herself but she is determined not to get married as she believes nobody could find a place in her heart except Sandeep.

*****THE END*****

www.ingramcontent.com/pod-product-compliance
Lightning Source LLC
LaVergne TN
LVHW061527200326
834410LV00009B/431